NODDY
GOES TO SCHOOL

HarperCollins *Children's Books*

First published in the UK by HarperCollins Children's Books in 2010

3 5 7 9 10 8 6 4 2
ISBN 978-0-00-735571-6

Printed and bound in China

NODDY
GOES TO SCHOOL

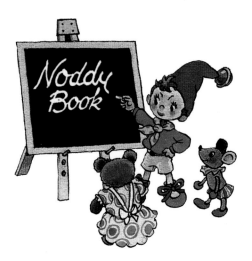

by Enid Blyton

Contents

NODDY WENT BRAVELY ON TO THE PLATFORM WITH AN
ENORMOUS BUNCH OF FLOWERS

—◦ 1 ◦—
NODDY'S SUCH A CLEVER FELLOW

ONE fine morning Noddy went to his little garage and opened the door.

"Hallo, little car!" he said. "You look rather dirty. I'll give you a wash."

"Well, mind you wash behind its ears!" called a cheeky little voice. Noddy turned round and saw a small girl monkey behind him.

"Just you tell me where a car's ears are!" said Noddy. "You silly monkey!"

"Under its bonnet, of course," said the toy monkey, grinning. "That's where *my* mother's ears are – under her bonnet."

Noddy couldn't think what to say to that. He was sure his car had no ears, even if it did have a bonnet. "You go away," he said to the little monkey. "And don't come bothering me. I'm going to wash my car."

The little monkey didn't go away. She just stayed, and watched Noddy get out the hose and begin to wash his car.

"When are you going to clean its teeth and brush its hair?" asked the cheeky monkey presently.

"I'll wash *your* face and clean *your* teeth first!" said Noddy fiercely, and he turned the hose on to the monkey. The water splashed into her face and made her yell.

Mrs Tubby Bear came over from next door and laughed. "That just serves the cheeky monkey right," she said. "She's a scamp. She keeps coming and knocking at my door and then running away. It was clever of you to wash her face for her so suddenly!"

Noddy felt pleased. He watched the monkey running down the street, water dripping from her naughty little face.

"Your car looks beautiful, Noddy," said Mrs Tubby. "Really, it's the best-kept car in Toyland."

Noddy felt pleased all over again. He began to polish his little car with a leather. My word, how it shone!

He thought of a little song as he polished his car.

"Oh, dear little car
I really must say
You're the best little car
In Toyland today.

"You hoot very loud,
You go along fine,
I feel very glad
Because you are mine!"

"Dear me," said Mrs Tubby Bear, "how clever you are, little Noddy. The songs you make up out of your little wooden head! I never knew anyone so clever. You must sing your new song to Mr Tubby."

So Noddy sang his new song to Mr Tubby and Miss Fluffy Cat came to listen too and the milkman as well.

NODDY SANG HIS NEW SONG TO MR AND MRS TUBBY,
MISS FLUFFY CAT AND THE MILKMAN

"Very good," they all said, and the milkman tapped Noddy's little head. It nodded up and down madly.

"Wonderful!" said the milkman. "Perhaps if we all had heads that nodded like Noddy's *we'd* be able to make up songs too."

Noddy got into his car, feeling very pleased and proud. He hooted loudly. "I'm off! I shall earn a lot of money today because I'm so clever."

Off he went down the street. He saw Mrs Skittle hopping along and she called him.

"Noddy! Noddy! Please tale me to the station."

In she got and Noddy whizzed her away to the

station. They arrived just as the train was coming in.

"Oh, thank you, Noddy," said Mrs Skittle, and she paid him sixpence. "Really, you are a marvellous driver! So very quick – and how nice your car looks!"

"Yes, I'm a good driver," said Noddy, and away he went, hooting loudly at two bears from the Noah's Ark. "Out of the way, bears! Here comes little Noddy!"

Then the clockwork clown hailed him. "Hey, little Noddy! My clockwork's broken down. Will you take me to the doctor, and see if he can mend me?

Please drive slowly because a bit of my clockwork has come loose inside me, and it rattles if I go too fast."

"I can drive as slowly as a snail," said Noddy, and he did. The clown's inside didn't rattle at all and he was very pleased. He got out at the doctor's and paid Noddy sixpence.

"Thank you," he said. "You are a very, very good driver. You can drive slowly just as well as fast. I don't know what we should do without you, little Noddy."

"Well, it's lucky I came to live in Toyland," said Noddy, pleased, and he drove off. Another little song came into his head and he sang it loudly as he went.

"Oh, anyone can see
I'm as clever as can be.
My brains are very fine,
They're polished till they shine.
There isn't anybody
That's cleverer than Noddy!"

BIG-EARS IS VERY CROSS

NOW, not very long after that, Noddy's hat came off. It fell on the seat beside him, its bell tinkling loudly.

"What did you do that for?" said Noddy, to his hat. "Stay on my head, please."

He put his hat on again and pulled it down firmly over his hair. But in half a minute it slid off once more and this time it fell into the road.

Noddy stopped his car, got out and picked up his hat. He was cross. "There you go again!" he said. "What do you think you're doing, hat, taking yourself off my head without my asking you?"

He put it on once more, but it didn't seem as good a fit as usual. In fact, it slid off again almost at once and Noddy began to feel puzzled. Could a spell have got into it? A slip-off spell, perhaps?

He pulled the hat on so hard that it went down on his nose. But it began to slip off again very quickly. Noddy had to drive with one hand and hold on to his blue hat with the other. The bell stopped tinkling, too, which was very queer.

"I think I'd better go and tell Big-Ears about my hat," thought Noddy, in alarm. "What can be the matter? It doesn't seem big enough for me now, and the bell won't ring. I haven't been out in the rain so it can't have shrunk. Oh dear, it's off again. Really, hat, what's got into you today?"

He drove up to Big-Ears' little toadstool house. Big-Ears was his friend. He would be able to tell Noddy what was suddenly the matter with his hat.

Noddy remembered his newest song when he got to the little toadstool house. He thought he would sing it loudly, so Big-Ears would come out and say how clever he was!

So he began to sing the song, at the top of his voice.

"Oh, anyone can see
I'm clever as can be.
My brains are very fine,
They're. . ."

Big-Ears came suddenly out of his little house, and he didn't look at all pleased. He was frowning and that surprised Noddy because Big-Ears hardly ever frowned.

"Be quiet, Noddy," said Big-Ears. "What a silly song! Please stop at once. I don't want to hear a song like that."

Noddy was so surprised that he forgot to hold his hat on and it slipped off at once and fell to the ground.

"B-b-b-but Big-Ears — I *am* clever," said little Noddy, staring at Big-Ears. "Everybody says so. Mrs Tubby said so, and. . ."

"If you're going to talk like that, and grow all vain and proud and conceited, I don't want to know you," said Big-Ears, "You're NOT clever as can be, so don't you think it!"

And will you believe it, Big-Ears went inside his toadstool house and shut the door!

Noddy stood outside wailing, "Big-Ears! Oh, Big-Ears! Don't talk like that. I came to ask you about my hat. It's behaving badly."

The door opened again and Big-Ears looked out. "What's the

"BE QUIET, NODDY," SAID BIG-EARS. "I DON'T WANT TO
HEAR A SONG LIKE THAT"

matter with your hat?" he asked, still looking cross.

"Well, look," said Noddy, and he put it on. "It doesn't fit me any more. It's too small. And the bell won't ring."

"Ho!" said Big-Ears. "Ha ha! Ho! Serves you right. You've got a swollen head! That's what you've got – and you deserve it too."

"What's swollen head?" said little Noddy, in alarm. "Is it an illness?"

"Of course," said Big-Ears. "People who think they are very clever, and go about shouting and singing that they're as clever as can be, people who are vain and proud, why, they're the ones whose heads suddenly swell up – just like your head has. My, you do look funny, Noddy."

He took Noddy into his house and made him

look into the looking-glass there. Noddy stared in dismay. His head was certainly very big indeed. He looked most peculiar.

"And, of course, now that your head has swollen up with pride, your hat won't fit it," said Big-Ears. "It's much too small. And your bell won't ring because it's cross with you for getting a swollen head."

"Oh dear," said Noddy. "What can I do?"

"Stop thinking you are so clever," said Big-Ears. "You're not really, you know, Noddy. Why, you know perfectly well that you can't count more than twenty, and you don't know how to read big words yet. And you do very, very silly things sometimes."

"I don't," said Noddy, beginning to cry.

"You do," said Big-Ears. "It's a pity you have never been to school. Then you might understand things a bit better. School would be good for you."

"Shall I go to school then?" asked poor Noddy. "Will you like me again if I go to school? I won't be vain any more. I won't sing that song any more."

"I think it would be a VERY, VERY good idea if you went to school!" said Big-Ears. "Dear me, why didn't we think of that before?"

"Shall I like it?" asked Noddy. "Will my head stop swelling if I go?"

"My goodness, yes," said Big-Ears. "There's nothing like school for curing swollen heads. Then you will be able to wear your hat again, Noddy!"

"I'll go then," said Noddy. "I'll go tomorrow Big-Ears. Yes. I will!"

─◦ 3 ◦─

NODDY GOES TO SCHOOL

SO the very next day, off went Noddy to school. He went in his little car, but he couldn't wear his hat because his head was still too big for it.

The school mistress was a plump little doll with a bonnet and shawl, and she wore big glasses on her nose. Noddy felt rather scared of her.

"Ah – it's little Noddy, isn't it?" said the teacher, smiling at him. "I'm Miss Prim. It's time you came to me, little Noddy. You've got a lot to learn!"

"Oh dear – have I?" said Noddy, alarmed. "Where do I sit?"

"Over there," said Miss Prim. "Between that little girl monkey and the little doll. Sit up straight, and don't talk."

Noddy took his seat. The girl monkey was the same one who had come into his garden the day before and asked him if he was going to wash behind his car's ears. She made a face at Noddy.

"I'll pay you out for soaking me with your hose!" she whispered. Noddy didn't answer. He didn't want to talk and get into trouble straight away.

"Now, we will have a number lesson," said Miss Prim. "Who can say the two times table?"

A small teddy bear got up at once, waving his paw. "I can, I can. One two is two, two twos are four. . ."

And then he stopped, and couldn't go on. Miss Prim looked at Noddy. "Do *you* know any tables?" she asked.

Little Noddy didn't know that she meant number tables, like one two is two. He thought she meant real tables.

"Yes. I know one table very well," he said. "It's my little table at home. I'll tell you about it. It stands in the middle of the floor, and it has a cloth on, and. . ."

Everybody began to laugh and laugh. Even Miss Prim laughed. "No, no," she said, "that's not the kind of table I mean, Noddy. Stop laughing everyone. Clara Kitten, stand up and sing a song."

Noddy felt quite ashamed when everyone laughed at him. Oh dear – perhaps he wasn't so very clever after all!

Clara Kitten sang a little song, and everyone clapped. Noddy put up his hand.

"Please, Miss Prim, I can sing a song too."

"Well, sing me 'Jack and Jill went up the hill'," said Miss Prim.

"I don't know that one," said Noddy. "But I know one all about myself."

"Oh, *anyone* can sing songs about themselves," said Miss Prim. "We don't bother to hear those, Noddy. Dear, dear - to think you don't even know 'Jack and Jill'. Where's the clockwork mouse? Oh, there you are, little mouse. Now – what can *you* sing?"

"The only song I know is about a pussy-cat who frightened a little mouse under a chair," said the clockwork mouse. "And I don't like it."

"Let's do some writing, let's do some writing," called out a little pink dog. "I know how to spell 'bone', I do really."

"Come up to the blackboard and write then," said Miss Prim. The pink toy dog went up proudly and wrote BONE in very good letters.

"Splendid," said Miss Prim. "Noddy, you come up and write something *you* like to eat."

Now Noddy could only write one word and that was his own name. So he wrote that. This is how he wrote it.

Noddy

"Why – I asked you to write something you like to *eat* - and you've written your own name!" said Miss Prim.

"Perhaps he likes to nibble at himself," called

NODDY COULD ONLY WRITE ONE WORD AND THAT WAS
HIS OWN NAME. SO HE WROTE THAT

out the girl monkey, and everyone laughed.

"That's quite enough, Martha Monkey," said Miss Prim. "And stop putting your foot on Clara Kitten's tail, please."

"I'm not putting my foot on her tail – she keeps putting her tail under my foot," said Martha Monkey.

"Oooh, you storyteller," said the kitten. "Miss Prim, she's a storyteller. Wherever I put my tail she puts her foot."

"Well, wrap it round your middle," said Miss Prim. "Martha Monkey, go outside the door."

"Oh no!" wailed the little monkey. Noddy

wondered why she didn't want to go. Surely she wasn't frightened to go outside by herself?

"Well, I'll let you off this time," said Miss Prim. "You needn't go outside now – but the very next time I have to speak to you, out you will go."

"Miss Prim, *I'll* go outside for you," cried Noddy, thinking it would be nice to do something for Miss Prim, and make her think he was a good toy.

"Noddy, people only go outside as a punishment for being naughty," said Miss Prim. "Surely you don't want me to punish you, when you haven't done anything wrong?"

Everyone laughed. Dear, dear, what a little silly Noddy was, to be sure!

Then the class had to get up to do a little dance, and poor Noddy didn't know how to do it at all. He watched the others kicking up their legs, this way and that, and he suddenly kicked up his too, just to show that he could.

"Ooooh! Noddy kicked me!" cried the clockwork mouse. "Ooooh, Miss Prim, he kicked me – look, he's kicked my key right out of my back!"

"I didn't mean to!" cried Noddy. "He got in my way just as I was kicking up my feet."

"I really think you had better go and stand in the corner, Noddy, till we've finished dancing," said Miss Prim.

Well, wasn't that dreadful? There is poor little Noddy standing in the corner, crying big tears on the floor. He doesn't feel a bit clever. He is sure now that his brains are not polished till they shine. He doesn't really think he's got any brains at all!

"Playtime, playtime!" called Miss Prim suddenly, and Noddy came out of his corner. Oh *what* a good thing! He did not know to do *this*, anyway. He knew how to play!

—◦ 4 ◦—
WORK HARD, LITTLE NODDY

NODDY went to see Big-Ears after school. He drove to the little toadstool house feeling rather sad. Big-Ears was waiting for him.

"Why, Noddy, what's happened?" said Big-Ears, as soon as he saw him. "Your head isn't nearly so big!"

"Isn't it really?" said Noddy, feeling it. "Oh, perhaps I can get my hat on again then."

But no, he couldn't. His head was still too swollen. What a pity!

"Still, it is certainly going down," said Big-Ears. "School must be doing you good. How did you get on?"

"Not very well," said Noddy, looking gloomy.

"I didn't really know anything – not as much as the clockwork mouse. I'm sorry I thought I was clever now, Big-Ears."

"Aha! If you go on thinking *that*, your head will soon be the right size," said Big-Ears, pleased. "Let me have your hat, Noddy. It will get dirty if you keep carrying it about, and you can't possibly wear it on your head yet. I'll hang it up on my peg – just here, look – and you shall have it again when your head is the right size."

"Big-Ears, teach me how to dance, and to sing 'Jack and Jill' and to write something," begged Noddy. "I don't want everyone to laugh at me again."

"Well, you shall do homework," said Big-Ears. "I will write you out some words to copy in your best writing, and I will show you how to do a proper little dance and how to add up."

"We didn't have adding up," said Noddy,

in alarm. "I can't add up. I can't add down either."

"You can. Just listen now. Suppose I give you two apples, and I give Martha Monkey one, how many apples would you have between you?"

"I know the answer to that," said Noddy, gloomily. "We wouldn't have any apples between us – Martha Monkey would take the lot!"

"Don't be silly," said Big-Ears. "Now do this sum – it's adding up again. Suppose there were three cats in my garden, and a dog came to join them, how many animals would we see out of my window?"

"One dog," said Noddy. "Because all the cats would run away."

"Dear me – you've got very queer brains," said Big-Ears. "But I don't think you've got quite *enough* brains, Noddy."

"No, I haven't," said Noddy, nodding his head. "I'll get some more. I've got a shilling in my money box. I'll go and buy some more brains this very day."

"You can't buy brains. You can only grow them," said Big-Ears. "And they don't grow in gardens either, so don't ask me if you can buy brain-seeds to plant. Now, here is some writing for you to copy when you get home. And just watch this little dance, and practise it at home too."

Big-Ears did a nice little dance and Noddy watched him. "Yes, I can do that," he said. "But I'd better go now, because it's getting late."

He drove back to his little house and went indoors. Oh dear – he hadn't any paper to write his homework on. Never mind – he would write it on the floor! He could clean it off afterwards.

So he wrote all over the floor. Then, because it was rather uncomfortable kneeling down for so long, writing on the floor, Noddy thought he would stretch his legs and dance.

So he danced, and while he was dancing somebody peeped in at the window. It was little Master Tubby Bear from next door.

"Noddy! Whatever are you doing, dancing all by yourself?" he said. "Can I come in and dance too?"

Then little Tubby came in and you should just have seen the two of them dancing together. At last they were very tired and they sat down, panting.

"Tubby, you go to school too – can you please teach me something?" asked Noddy. Tubby looked at him.

"Well – I could teach you how to growl," he said. "I can growl beautifully - listen." He pressed himself in the middle, and a growl came out at once.

"Oh yes – that's fine," said Noddy. "I'd like to learn how to do that. I put my hand just here, you say, Tubby?"

"Yes. Now press your little wooden tummy, and make it growl," said Tubby.

But what a pity – no matter how hard Noddy pressed his little wooden middle, it wouldn't growl!

"Well – never mind – perhaps we could get Clara Kitten here and let her teach you how to walk along a branch of a tree balancing with your tail," said Tubby.

"But I haven't got a tail," said Noddy. "Teach me

YOU SHOULD JUST HAVE SEEN NODDY AND LITTLE TUBBY
DANCING TOGETHER

how to grow one first,"

"I don't know that," said Tubby. "Noddy, I'll come with you to school tomorrow and you can sit next to me, instead of that horrid Martha Monkey. She nearly got sent outside today, didn't she? She's always getting into trouble."

Noddy made up his mind that Miss Prim would never, never send *him* outside. He looked at all the writing he had done on the floor. "You'd better go now," he said to Tubby. "I must practise some more writing. I've still got the walls to write on – it's lucky they are washable! Goodbye."

Tubby went, and Noddy began writing again, all over the walls this time. Work hard, little Noddy – you'll be top of the school one day!

NODDY ISN'T VERY CLEVER

NODDY soon began to enjoy school. He worked very hard indeed, and Miss Prim was pleased with him. Little Tubby Bear sat next to him and helped him a lot.

Each morning there was marching round the room, and the leader always had a drum to beat – boom-boom-boom, boom-diddy-boom. How Noddy wished and wished he could be the leader and have the drum.

And then one morning Miss Prim called him out in front and gave him the drum!

"You've done such a good week's work that you shall be the leader of the marching and bang the drum!" she said.

Noddy was so pleased. He marched proudly round the room banging the drum. Boom-boom-boom, diddy-boom.

And then another day he did such a beautiful painting of Little Tubby Bear that Miss Prim pinned it up on the wall for everyone to see.

He went to tell Big-Ears about the drum.

"I banged the drum today," he said. "Like this Big-Ears, boom-boom, boom-diddy-boom. And I made a louder boom-boom than anyone else ever does."

"Now don't you begin to boast," said Big-Ears, at once. "Your head is going down nicely, and you don't want it to swell up again, do you?"

"No, I don't," said Noddy, feeling his head. "it almost feels right, Big-Ears. Shall I try on my dear little hat again, and see if the bell rings?"

"No," said Big-Ears "you aren't cured yet." Noddy went to tell Big-Ears about his beautiful painting two days later — but he didn't boast about it, and Big-Ears was pleased.

"You're getting much nicer," he said. "I'm quite glad I know you, Noddy. Are you still bottom of the school?"

"No, I'm creeping up," said Noddy. "I'm better than the clockwork mouse now, and better than Martha Monkey, and better than the pink dog. But I'll never, never win a prize, Big-Ears, so please don't expect it."

"No, I won't expect it," said Big-Ears. "Miss Prim always gives us a concert at the end of term, and you'll be in it — but I'm afraid you won't win a prize."

"No. I'm not very clever after all," said Noddy sadly. "And I really did think I was, but I do drive my car well, don't I, Big-Ears?"

"You shouldn't even say *that*!" said Big-Ears.

"Let other people say it for you!"

And oh dear – will you believe it, poor Noddy ran into a tree on the way home and knocked it down! It belonged to the Wobbly Man, and he was very cross indeed. He wobbled after Noddy

at once. "I'm sorry, I'm sorry, I'm sorry!" called Noddy in alarm. "Your tree got in my way!"

"You're a very bad driver to let trees get in your way," said the Wobbly Man. "Why don't you hoot at them, silly?"

"They don't take any notice of hooting," said Noddy, putting the tree up again. "There – the tree's quite right all right. Don't make such a fuss."

"If you talk to me like that I'll wobble all over your car," said the Wobbly Man and Noddy drove away in alarm. Oh dear – perhaps he wasn't such a good driver after all!

"I wish I had my little blue hat back," he thought. "I don't feel right without it. What a dreadful thing to be so vain that my head swelled up and I couldn't wear my dear little hat. I do miss its tinkle-tinkle-tinkle."

And then, dear me, Noddy got a cold. "A-tish-oo! A TISH-oo! WHOOOSHOOO!"

"It's because you keep driving out in your car without your hat," said Mrs Tubby Bear, looking over the fence. "What's happened to your nice blue hat? Put it on, Noddy."

"I got a swollen head and it wouldn't fit me any more," said Noddy sadly. "Big-Ears is keeping it for me till my head fits it again."

"Dear, dear a swollen head is a shocking thing," said Mrs Tubby. "Well, you certainly must get a hat, Noddy. I'll lend you one of mine."

She made him put on a little bonnet of hers,

trimmed with flowers. But, oh dear, how Martha Monkey and the others laughed at him. He wouldn't wear it the second day.

Tubby Bear played a trick on him the next day. He came out with what looked liked a dear little hat with a pattern on it.

"Here you are," he said. "Wear this, Noddy."

"A-tish-oo! Thank you," said Noddy, and put it on. But oh dear, it wasn't a hat, it was the little lamp-shade out of Tubby's bedroom, and Noddy didn't know it. Oh, Noddy, Noddy!

Well, of course, everyone laughed still more, and Martha Monkey said she would lend him a plant-pot to wear, in case the lamp shade wasn't warm enough. Noddy was very cross with Tubby and the cheeky monkey.

He took off the lamp shade and pressed it down so hard on Martha Monkey's head that she couldn't get it off, and she went home crying with the shade stuck down over her nose.

Mrs Tubby Bear saw her going down the street

NODDY TOOK OFF THE LAMP-SHADE AND PRESSED IT DOWN
HARD ON MARTHA MONKEY'S HEAD

and was most astonished to see one of her own lamp-shades on the little monkey's head. She ran after her and pulled it off. Then she gave her a good telling off which really *Tubby* ought to have had. Martha Monkey howled.

"It serves you right," said little Noddy, who was watching. "You're a nasty, horrid little tease, and you've often got me into trouble. Now you know what it feels like!"

Then Martha Monkey ran after Noddy and he fled.

"A-tish-oo!" Oh, if only he had his own dear little blue hat back again with its tinkling bell!

—◦🌀 6 🌀◦—

THE DAY OF THE CONCERT

THE day of the school concert drew nearer. What fun it was going to be! Everyone was doing something.

"I'm doing a sailor dance," said the sailor doll.

"We're singing a skittle song," said the skittles. "And then Billy Ball is going to roll on the stage and knock us all down! We're going to yell like anything."

"I'm singing a quacking song," said the toy duck proudly.

"I'm saying a poem about a sweep," said Martha Monkey. "I've got a sweep's brush too.

If I don't like quacking songs, Dilly Duck,
I'll sweep you away with my brush."

"You won't," said Noddy, who was very fond
of the little toy duck. "I'll see you don't! I'll hide
your brush!"

"I'm doing a nice growly song," said the little
Tubby Bear. "I've been practising it at home."

"Oh — so *that's* what you've been doing," said
Noddy. "I kept hearing you every night. I thought
you must be ill."

"We're doing a fairy dance," said the two fairy
dolls.

"I shall clap and clap!" said Noddy, who
thought the fairy dolls were just about the
prettiest dolls he had ever seen. "And I shall nod
my head like anything."

"What are *you* going to do, Noddy," asked Clara Kitten.

"Nothing," said Noddy, sadly. "Miss Prim says I'm not good enough to sing. And I can't dance well, because my left foot gets in the way of my right one. And I can't say a poem because I keep forgetting what comes next. And I can't quack or growl, though I've tried. I can only nod my head."

"You're not very clever," said Martha Monkey. "Not at all clever. Fancy not doing anything at the concert!"

"You won't get a single prize," said the sailor doll.

"I can't help it," said Noddy, hanging his head. "I *could* sing one of my own songs, but people would think me very vain if I did. And I'm trying not to be, so that I can get back my dear little blue hat with the tinkling bell."

Well, the day of the concert came at last, and everyone arrived to hear the toys and see them. Mrs Duck came to hear Dilly Duck, Mr and Mrs Monkey came to see Martha Monkey, and Mrs Skittle came to hear all the little skittles singing. There was quite a crowd in the schoolroom.

Miss Prim had a platform put up at one end of the room. Her pupils were longing to begin the concert, and at last it was time. They all came on together and sang the opening song. Noddy too. Big-Ears was there, and he waved to him. Dear old Big-Ears – how nice of him to come, even though Noddy wasn't doing anything by himself at the concert, and wasn't even having a prize!

You would have loved that concert! It was wonderful. Dilly Duck quacked her little song and everyone clapped. Look at her, isn't she sweet?

Martha Monkey was a great success, and swept a pretend chimney so hard when she said her poem that she almost swept the piano off the platform.

THEY ALL CAME ON TOGETHER AND SANG THE

OPENING SONG

Little Tubby Bear was clapped so loudly that he had to come on and do his growling song all over again. Noddy clapped him till his hands nearly wore out!

At the end the little clockwork mouse was supposed to take a bunch of flowers and give them to Miss Prim with a nice little speech. But

just at the last minute he said he couldn't do it!

"I can't! I can't! I'm too shy! I shall forget what I've got to say! I shall swallow my whiskers! I shall fall over my tail!" he squealed.

"Well, somebody else must do it then," said Martha Monkey. "I can't. I'm no good at that sort of thing. Besides, I don't know the speech that the clockwork mouse was going to make."

Nobody knew it except the clockwork mouse. Oh dear − whatever were they to do?

"Well − I do like Miss Prim so much," said Noddy, at last. "I can't bear her not to have her flowers, and a nice little speech. *I'll* do it − and if I make a muddle of it, well, I just can't help it!"

EVERYTHING COMES RIGHT

SO Noddy went bravely on to the platform all by himself, with an ENORMOUS bunch of flowers. What was he to say? Oh dear, do think of something, Noddy!

And, will you believe it, a little song came into his head, all about Miss Prim! What a lucky thing. Noddy sang it out at the top of his voice.

> *"Hurrah for Miss Prim,*
> *She is perfectly sweet,*
> *From the hair on her head*
> *To the toes on her feet.*
> *She teaches us sums,*
> *And everyone's happy*
> *Whenever she comes!*
> *Three cheers for Miss Prim,*
> *Hurrah and hooray,*
> *Our concert is over,*
> *That's all for today!"*

And then little Noddy went up to the surprised Miss Prim, bowed very low and gave her the flowers. She really was delighted.

Noddy went back behind the stage with the others. "How *did* you think of that song?" said the sailor doll. "It was *wonderful.*"

"Fancy singing it all out without making a mistake!" said Tubby. "Why, I've never even *heard* the song before!"

"Nor have I," said Noddy, feeling just as astonished as the others. "It came straight out of my head."

"Where did it get out?" asked the clockwork mouse, looking all round Noddy's wooden head.

"Well — from his *mouth* of course," said a skittle. "Don't be silly. Now hush — we've got to go down to our seats in the schoolroom — it's the prize giving! Ooooooh! I'm longing for my prize."

They all went down quietly to their places and sat down. Only Miss Prim was on the platform, and in front of her were piles of exciting-looking books — the prizes!

"Little Dilly Duck!" called Miss Prim, holding up a picture book. "A prize for learning to turn her toes in so nicely."

"The clockwork mouse, for being a fast runner," called Miss Prim, and up went the mouse proudly,

"Martha Monkey for trying so hard with her reading," said Miss Prim, and up went the little monkey. Everyone clapped loudly.

One by one all the pupils went up. Noddy felt sad that he had won no prize at all. If only he was clever at something! He sat close to Big-Ears and hoped that no one would notice he was the only person who hadn't won a prize.

But what was this? Miss Prim was calling out HIS name! Yes, it really was his name!

"Little Noddy! A prize for being such a dear little fellow! Little Noddy, come along up, please."

Noddy was so very surprised that he just sat and stared, his head nodding madly. A prize for *him*? It couldn't be.

"Go on up, Noddy," said Big-Ears, giving him a push. "Hurry! We want to clap you!"

And up went little Noddy, beaming all over his face, almost falling up the step in his hurry.

"There you are," said Miss Prim, smiling at him. "A prize for being such a dear little fellow."

UP WENT LITTLE NODDY TO RECEIVE HIS PRIZE

FROM MISS PRIM

You should have heard the clapping and cheering. Really, it was wonderful, and Big-Ears felt so proud of Noddy that he nearly got up and danced.

"You must come home to tea with me, Noddy," he said. "I'm so pleased about your prize. I've got a nice new chocolate cake, and we'll share it."

So they went home together, and Big-Ears put his arm round Noddy very proudly indeed. To think his friend had won such a very nice prize!

When Noddy got to Big-Ears' house, the very first thing he saw was his little blue hat hanging up on the peg.

"Oh dear – I DO wish I could wear it again," he said. "I don't feel *right* without it somehow."

Big-Ears took a good look at him. "Noddy, your head looks quite small again," he said. "I don't believe you're vain or proud any more. Are you?"

"Oh no," said Noddy. "I know quite well I'm not clever now. Why, I wasn't even properly in the concert. I didn't do anything by myself at all, except give the flowers to Miss Prim. I can't be vain now, Big-Ears."

"Then you can't be swollen-headed anymore," said Big-Ears. "Let's try on the hat."

He took it down. Noddy pulled it on his head – and it fitted! It really and truly fitted! And its bell tinkled loudly – jingle-jingle-jing!

"Oh, my head's gone back to its right size! I'm cured, I'm cured!" cried Noddy, and he took Big-Ears' hands and made him dance round in a ring. He sang loudly,

> *"Oh, now I'm happy as anything,*
> *I've got my hat with its jingle-jing,*
> *I won't be proud and I won't be vain,*
> *I've got my little hat back again."*

"I'm so glad," panted Big-Ears. "You're *such* a nice fellow, Noddy. I'm so glad!"

So are we, little Noddy. Have your chocolate cake and be happy. We'll see you again soon!